IGOR'S LAB OF FEAR

OOZE IS IT?

by Michael Dahl   illustrated by Igor Šinkovec

STONE ARCH BOOKS
a capstone imprint

Igor's Lab of Fear is published by Stone Arch Books
A Capstone Imprint
1710 Roe Crest Drive, North Mankato, Minnesota 56003
www.capstonepub.com

Cataloging-in-Publication Data is available at the Library of Congress
website.
Hardcover ISBN: 978-1-4965-0457-9
Paperback ISBN: 978-1-4965-0461-6
Ebook ISBN: 978-1-4965-2322-8

SUMMARY: A group of friends drives to a private lake for nighttime
fishing when a meteor impacts nearby. Meteors can bring thousands
of dollars to those lucky enough to find them — after all, they're just
oozing with valuable minerals. But this one is oozing with something
else, too — something from the darkest corners of space.

DESIGNER: Kristi Carlson

Printed in China.
012016   009432R

TABLE OF CONTENTS

Who's there?!

What do you want?

Stand back, I say!
This dungeon is full
of danger!

Ah, it's
only you.

Forget what I said about my dungeon.

I was just having a little fun.

This is my laboratory, of course.

Yes, yes, it's just a science lab. Nothing more.

What's that in the cooler, you ask?

Hehe. Well, that's an interesting story . . .

CHAPTER ONE
FALLING SKIES

High above the deep, dark Canadian woods, a **METEOR** blazed through the sky.

"Look!" said Livia.

She and her friends, Zander and
Oscar, were riding in Oscar's truck.

They were driving to a quiet lake
for some late-night fishing.

Oscar pointed at the sky. "It's a meteor," he said.

A **SHOCK WAVE** rocked the truck.

"It crashed!" shouted Zander.

"It looked like it hit near **Dark Lake**," Oscar said.

Zander switched on the radio.

Several stations were already talking about the meteor.

"*A meteor crashed somewhere west of the town of Running Horse,*" said the radio announcer.

"Our town!" said Livia.

"See?" Oscar said. "I told you it was heading toward the lake."

Oscar stepped on the accelerator.

The pickup truck rocketed down the twisting road.

Up ahead, the woods glowed with an EERIE light.

CHAPTER TWO
THE METEOR

"Over there!" Zander cried, pointing.

Oscar hit the brakes. All three friends jumped out of the truck.

Zander led them through the trees toward the glow.

There was no breeze that night.
But Livia felt as if she was being
pulled toward the eerie light.

Suddenly, they stepped into a
clearing.

The trees had been smashed flat.

"The air is **hot**," Livia said.

They saw a huge crater in the middle of the clearing.

At the bottom of the crater was a large, glowing boulder.

Purple steam hissed off its rocky surface.

Zander swore under his breath.

Livia took a few steps toward the smoldering rock.

"Don't touch it!" Oscar said. "It might be dangerous. Or **RADIOACTIVE** or something."

The three friends stared at the meteor.

No one spoke.

CHAPTER THREE
PRICELESS

They decided to tell the police in Running Horse.

They climbed back into the truck. The engine roared. They raced away from the meteor site.

Livia turned on the radio again.

"Scientists have been tracking the valuable meteor through outer space," said the newscaster.

"Valuable?" Zander said.

"*The rare metals in the meteor could help scientific research,*" continued the newscaster. "*Anyone with information about —*"

Oscar turned the radio off.

"Valuable," he repeated.

The friends were silent. Each one was thinking about the meteor.

Then Livia said, "Maybe we shouldn't tell the **police** right away."

CHAPTER FOUR
MAKING PLANS

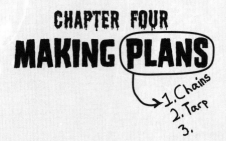

1. Chains
2. Tarp
3.

"The police will find it soon enough," Zander said. "When the sun rises, probably."

"So we'll get back here before dawn," Livia said.

"I'll bring some chains to haul out that rock," Oscar said.

"I'll get a tarp to cover it," said Livia.

"I'll bring a couple fire extinguishers," said Zander. "They might help cool it off."

They planned to take the meteor to Oscar's garage.

Then they would sell it to the scientists.

They drove back home to gather their tools. On the way, all they talked about was all the (money) they were going to make.

rich
Rich
RICH!!

Oscar dropped Livia off at her house.

He said they'd be back to pick her up in six hours.

After the truck pulled away, Livia didn't go inside.

She began to make another plan.

A **SECRET** plan.

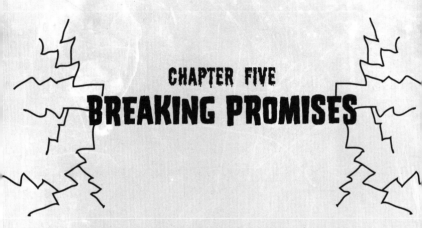

CHAPTER FIVE
BREAKING PROMISES

An hour later, Livia was riding her bike through the dark woods.

The closer she got to the purple glow, the faster her bike seemed to move.

When she reached the meteor, she slid off her backpack.

She pulled out the chisel and hammer she had taken from her father's toolshed.

She knelt down by the meteor and began to chisel.

Livia chipped off a large **CHUNK**.

She held it in her hands and smiled.

Now she would be rich.

Richer than her friends.

Richer than anyone she knew.

CRACK!

Someone else was in the woods with her.

Livia looked behind her.

Oscar stepped into the clearing.

"What are you doing here?" Livia asked.

"What are you doing here?" Oscar replied.

Zander jumped out from his hiding spot behind a tree. "So you're both _liars_ and thieves!" he said.

The three began fighting over the chunk of meteor.

Three hands gripped the rock.

No one would let go.

"Mine!" each one shouted. "Mine!"

The purple glow began to **PULSE**.

The air grew hot and wet.

Livia pointed at Zander. His hand and arm were turning purple.

Then they began to melt.

"Livia! Your legs!" shouted Oscar.

Livia looked down.

The skin dripped from her legs like wax from a candle.

She watched her friends dissolve into purple slime.

The ooze crawled toward her.

Livia tried to scream, but her jaw had melted.

They only thought of themselves.

But in the end, they *stuck* together.
Like true friends.

Olivia, Oscar, and Zander.

Ooze is it. Get it?   Heh Heh
Heh Heh

Oh yes, I might have an antidote.

I suppose I could turn them back to normal. If I wanted to.

Ah, but they work so well together.

Such a good team. So very . . . *slick*.

Hehe.

PROFESSOR IGOR'S LAB NOTES

If you think that all space rocks are the same, you're dead wrong. There's lots of different kinds. Even *I* have trouble keeping them all straight, and I'm a professor! (Unofficially.)

Meteors are chunks of rock, metal, and ice. They're ejected from comets. Comets are big space rocks that orbit the sun and have visible tails. So in a way, meteors are kind of like comet poop. Hehe.

When Earth passes through a comet's trail of debris, a meteor shower occurs. The chunks of rock and metal that make up meteors enter the atmosphere as meteoroids. And if those meteoroids stay intact and hit the Earth's surface, they're called meteorites.

Take a good look at the moon and you'll see tons of craters left by meteorites. Because the moon's surface doesn't change much over time, many of those craters are older than your great-great-great-grandmother. Older than me, even!

To put it a way you kids will understand better: your face is kind of like the Earth's surface, bacteria is the meteorite that impacts your face, and your pimples are the craters!

GLOSSARY

ACCELERATOR (ak-SEL-uh-ray-tohr)—a pedal in a vehicle that is pressed to increase speed

ANTIDOTE (AN-ti-doht)—a substance that stops the harmful effects of a poison

CHISEL (CHIZ-uhl)—a metal tool with a flat, sharp end that is used to cut and shape

DUNGEON (DUHN-juhn)—a dark underground prison

EERIE (EER-ee)—strange, creepy, or mysterious

LABORATORY (LAB-ruh-tohr-ee)—a room or building with special equipment used for science

METEOR (MEE-tee-er)—a piece of rock or metal that burns brightly in the sky as it falls from outer space into the Earth's atmosphere

PULSE (PUHLSS)—a brief increase in light

RADIOACTIVE (ray-dee-oh-AK-tiv)—having or producing a powerful and dangerous form of energy (called radiation)

SMOLDERING (SMOHL-dur-ing)—burning slowly without flames but usually with smoke

DISCUSSION QUESTIONS

1. Which one of the three friends in this story do you think is most to blame for what happened to them — Olivia, Oscar, or Zander? Why?

2. In this story, one of the friends is older than the other two. Which one do you think is the oldest? (Hint: what can a 16-year-old do legally that a 13-year-old can't? It happens in this story.)

3. Is there a moral to this story? What do you think it is? Discuss it.

WRITING PROMPTS

1. If you could have a secret lab like Professor Igor that was filled with strange objects, what kinds of things would you want to keep there? Write a list of oddities you'd keep bottled up.

2. Do you think we can trust Professor Igor? Why or why not? Write a paragraph trying to convince others that your opinion is correct.

3. Write two paragraphs about what it's like to be trapped in the ooze along with two of your best friends. How does it feel? How will you turn yourself back to normal? Write about it.

AUTHOR BIOGRAPHY

Michael Dahl, the author of the Library of Doom, Dragonblood, and Troll Hunters series, has a long list of things he's afraid of: dark rooms, small rooms, damp rooms (all of which describe his writing area), storms, rabid squirrels, wet paper, raisins, flying in planes (especially taking off, cruising, and landing), and creepy dolls. He hopes that by writing about fear he will eventually be able to overcome his own. So far it isn't working. But he is afraid to stop, so he continues to write. He lives in a haunted house in Minneapolis, Minnesota.

ILLUSTRATOR BIOGRAPHY

Igor Sinkovec was born in Slovenia in 1978. As a kid he dreamt of becoming a truck driver — or failing that, an astronaut. As it turns out, he got stuck behind a drawing board, so sometimes he draws semi trucks and space shuttles. Igor makes his living as an illustrator. Most of his work involves illustrating books for kids. He lives in Ljubljana, Slovenia.